OUR WORLD

Praise for the Book

Abraham Lincoln once said, 'If I had more time, I would have written a shorter letter.' And I just spent sixteen words quoting Lincoln to appreciate (albeit in a roundabout way) the thought and time spent by this family of authors in bringing us the joy of short-form reading!

Puneet Sikka
Advertising professional and Founder of ARTEREE

The drabbles written by the family of three generations are very interesting and entertaining. After a tiring day of work from home and work at home, I took the manuscript to bed with me. I thoroughly enjoyed the stories and felt rejuvenated. Some drabbles brought a smile to my lips, others a tear or a chuckle, still others gave an element of surprise, shock or happiness. It is amazing how a book can encompass a myriad of emotions! My congratulations and best wishes to the three authors.

Dr Alka Behari
Professor of Education, University of Delhi

Between what is said and what is unsaid, this book of Drabbles compels and invites readers to imagine, think and co-create the stories in a way that they linger on, long after the experience. To further add refreshingly different perspectives to this quaint form of storytelling, the 86 dramatic drabbles are presented by authors spanning three generations: Bishan Sahai, the grandfather, Ruchi Ranjan, the mother, and Ishika Ranjan, the 15-year-old daughter. Drabble on!

Harimohan Paruvu
writer and executive coach

I am proud of what you have become, Ishika. Your drabbles are clever. I enjoy how you can write in different genres: legends, sci-fi and fiction, and develop a little story with so few words. I remember you in third grade, working hard on your stories and am happy to hear that you are continuing. Keep sharing your stories with the world!

Summer Thompson
Literacy coach and former teacher of creative writing at
MLK School, Cambridge, MA

It gives me immense pleasure to learn that a set of stories written by Ishika Ranjan is to be published. In the three years that I was associated with her as a teacher of English Language and Literature, I have always enjoyed reading her stories and essays. Her exceptionally good writing skills reflect an instinctive grasp of the language as well as a flair for creating distinct and strong characters. She possesses the ability to write wonderfully creative stories that are heartfelt, moving the reader immensely. Her sense of humour shines through when she opts to give an unexpected twist to one of her stories. Her essays are generally presented with clarity of thought, often persuasive enough to win the reader over to her point of view. Her style is imaginative and creative, blending dialogue and narration effectively to create stories that are sure to interest readers of various age groups.

In her 100-word stories she has engaged with a range of themes, from science fiction to dreams and even to her memories of the school she studied in. I wish her good luck in all that she undertakes.

Naina Joseph
Teacher of English, Vidyaranya High School, Hyderabad

OUR WORLD

A Symphony of Drabbles

by THREE GENERATIONS

BISHAN SAHAI   RUCHI RANJAN   ISHIKA RANJAN

RUPA

Published by
Rupa Publications India Pvt. Ltd 2020
7/16, Ansari Road, Daryaganj
New Delhi 110002

Sales Centres:
Allahabad Bengaluru Chennai
Hyderabad Jaipur Kathmandu
Kolkata Mumbai

This is a work of fiction. Names, characters, places and incidents are
either the product of the author's imagination or are used fictitiously and
any resemblance to any actual person, living or dead, events or locales is
entirely coincidental.

ISBN: 978-93-9035-614-0

Ninth impression 2022

15 14 13 12 11 10 9

The moral right of the authors has been asserted.

Printed in India

In remembrance of our loved ones:
Shri L.S. Narain, Shri Gopal Behari and
Smt. Jyotsna Sahai
and
fondly dedicated to Ishika's Dadi and Nani

Contents

Foreword   xi
Acknowledgements   xv
Preface   xvi

1. Chee Chee   1
2. The Rainbow Girl   2
3. The Modern Mummy   3
4. Longing   4
5. The Racy Drive   5
6. Terra Incognita   6
7. Call of the Wild   7
8. How the Birds Got Their Colours   8
9. The Cheerleaders   9
10. What Hurts Most   10
11. Eccentric Enigma   13
12. The Birthday Spa   14
13. Best Friend No More   15
14. Ecstasy   16
15. Hide and Seek   17
16. Metamorphosis   18
17. Custodian of the Forest   21
18. Flash of Lightning   22

19. The Musical Family — 23
20. Prudence Jayate — 24
21. Eggcelent — 25
22. Baithak of the Mynas — 27
23. Dare to be Different — 28
24. The Battlefield — 29
25. Dancing Queen — 30
26. A Whole New World — 31
27. Good Vibes Only — 32
28. Real vs. Reel — 33
29. The Wider Lens — 35
30. Wait for God — 36
31. The Whistle, A Boy — 37
32. Playing with Panthers — 38
33. Believe It or Not — 39
34. The Guest — 41
35. Trapped — 42
36. Pawsome — 43
37. Midnight Rendezvous — 44
38. Snakes and Ladders — 47
39. Adventures for the Young — 48
40. Meri Ganga Maili — 49
41. Role Reversal — 50
42. The Yeti — 51
43. School Alone — 52
44. Standing Firm — 55

45. Mister Sinister   56
46. The Early Riser   57
47. Life Can Never be the Same Again   58
48. Animal Empire Strikes Back   61
49. Against All Odds   62
50. Deep Sea Terror   63
51. Detox   64
52. Forever Young   65
53. As Bright as the Fireflies   67
54. Much Ado About Nothing   68
55. The Precious Pearl   69
56. Challenged by Covid   70
57. Daughters as Daughters   73
58. Bruno's Day Out   74
59. Knock Knock   77
60. Machines May Lie   78
61. Short-Cut   79
62. The Director's Cut   81
63. Dead Man Alive   82
64. Whose Script Is It?   83
65. The Solitary Window   85
66. Masked   86
67. Trick or Treat   87
68. The Walls of Silence   88
69. Enhancing the Taste   89
70. Finding the Warrior Within   90

71. The Byte — 91
72. The Mesh of Strings — 92
73. Dark — 93
74. Dev and His Companion — 95
75. Building Blocks — 96
76. Never Give Up — 97
77. The Ritual — 98
78. Holding On — 99
79. Shop Right — 100
80. Necklace or Noose? — 101
81. The Silent Night — 102
82. #Instafamous — 103
83. The Mysterious Mr Red — 104
84. More Than a Home — 105
85. Paris Pre-empted — 107
86. Hope — 108

Just a small teaspoon of sea water holds the entire DNA of the ocean. The same may be said of us humankind, where even the minutest of hair strands, nails or any body part carries the complete genome sequence of an entire body. In simple, short words, the very subsistence of our life's story depends upon the tiniest of the almost invisible molecules, which then develops to become mega-success stories of our lives.

Hindustan's *vedas*, *shastras* and *granths* are filled with literature that modern science has still to grapple with.

Thousands of years ago, Sushruta recorded the equipment he used for carrying out plastic surgery. Reading a single line of the text encouraged me to read the entire scripture. Likewise, when NASA learnt of Guru Nanak's statement suggesting that the sun in our universe was not stationary but in motion, at its own steady pace, the team researched and published papers, indirectly admitting what Guru Nanak had already stated in his hymns. Small, therefore, is not only beautiful and powerful, it is also that much more difficult to envisage and collate.

Honestly, I wasn't even aware of the inconsequential sounding word, 'drabble', or what it was; but brevity, I knew, could test the author's infinite ability and provide him with powerful wings to express his imagination within a confined space. I began reading the manuscript, casually at first, but ended up finishing half of the unputdownable script before realising it was well past midnight. Early morning at the golf course, I was barely able to swing my clubs. It wasn't due to lack of sleep–a thought had gotten into my head and had stayed etched on the mind.

By the time my driver dropped me home, I had completed the rest of the short stories. Afterwards, standing under the shower, I knew exactly how this brilliant idea could unshackle the vice-like grip of the digital mediums' control on the minds of the younger generation. Today, we are all used to short texts and like to express views which are limited to about 140 odd words. But these short texts, when arranged and compiled into a story, leave an exciting, meaningful gatha. In its wake, the symphony ignites a desire, fuels an urge to indulge deeper and converts an ordinary mortal into a lover of books.

Drabbling, therefore, has that irrefutable,

magnetic power to be the booster for the upcoming generation. This book, a first-of-its-kind in India, could act as a positive catalyst to encourage the dying art of putting on our thinking caps and brainstorming a complex matter. Ironically, its absence is what now often leads to quick-decision-making that, when it goes wrong, makes even a nation as big as India repent at its own leisure.

My best wishes and heartiest congratulations to the grandfather, the mother and the daughter for bringing back... HOPE!

Harinder Sikka,
bestselling author of *Calling Sehmat* and *Vichhoda*, producer of the multiple National Award-winning film *Nanak Shah Fakir*

Acknowledgements

No book can be published through the sole efforts of the authors. While the three of us take credit as authors, there are many others who have helped us on the way. We would like to acknowledge them.

First and foremost, we thank our family and friends for their good wishes and blessings. We extend special gratitude to Jayesh for introducing us to the new concept of drabble writing and to Alka (Ishika's aunt) for encouraging her at every step. Thanks to Ruchi's namesake—Ruchi, for being a supportive friend always.

We thank the teachers of Vidyaranya High School for nurturing the writing talent within Ishika and for their motivation. Thanks are due to Mrs Summer Thompson and Mr Berkowitz, teachers of creative writing, Grade 3 (year 2012) at the MLK Junior School Cambridge, Massachusetts, for enabling Ishika to let her imagination and creativity freely flow.

Some of the drabbles are complemented either by an illustration or by a photograph. We thank the artists, Debabrata Biswas and Rahamtul Haq for infusing detail in the stories with their beautiful work.

We are happy to place into your hands a different kind of book. A drabble is a relatively new form of writing, not yet very popular in India. The concept of drabbles is said to have originated in the 1980s, in the UK Science Fiction Fandom, with the Birmingham University SF Society taking the lead.

If you are wondering what is a drabble: it is a story written in precisely 100 words—not a word more, not a word less.

Writing a drabble is both challenging and fun. Reading a drabble is a pleasure. It is ideal for when one is in the mood for a light and quick read. For instance, while commuting, while waiting at the railway station or at the airport or while taking a break from serious work. It can be read anytime, anywhere. Composing a drabble is a unique experience. Not only does the author have to be careful with the form—rendered in exactly 100 words—but also endeavour to tell an interesting story. And a story which has a beginning, a middle and an end!

In the year 2016, we came across a format called Lilliput Stories on an online community. The idea of writing drabbles got initiated at that point of time. Ruchi's husband, Jayesh, happens to be a member of a book club. Theme-based discussions are a hallmark of this society, and it was during one of these meetings hosted by us, that Jayesh suggested that we engage in drabble writing. It turned out to be a novel idea for all present. For the first time, we tried our hand at writing a story—exactly in 100 words. Ishika was twelve-years-old then and used to write long stories. One of her stories was shortened to suit the 100-word format. It took a long time to edit it to fit the form, longer than it would have taken her to write that very story! A humorous anecdote was shared by the grandfather at the meet, which was also in the form of a drabble.

After that, we penned down a few more, and then forgot about them for months altogether. Ruchi, in particular, would write a drabble at least once every year as a tribute to her late father-in-law, a journalist, who too had a passion for writing and had encouraged his daughter-in-law in every way. We were motivated by family and friends to continue writing and to compile the drabbles; they saw a flair in us for this kind of an exercise. We realised that the three of us (that is, the three generations) *together* could compose varied and engaging drabbles, worthy of being published in the form of a book.

However, this became feasible only recently in 2020, while the world has been hit by the pandemic. We want to impress upon our readers that in the midst of such a grave situation, there is a need for everyone to rise above negativity and not be deterred by the existence of the novel Coronavirus.

Our World: A Symphony of Drabbles by Three Generations, is a compilation of eighty-six drabbles, from a family of three generations—the grandfather, the mother and the daughter. Every drabble is a world in itself. The number 86 holds a special significance for us as we, fans of the legendary Ruskin Bond, celebrate his 86th birthday this year. 2020 also marks the 70th year of the great author's writing journey.

We have covered a plethora of interesting stories, spanning across several genres. Some stories are funny and entertaining, some are quixotic, others skirt around tales of soft sci-fi and adventure, while others evoke feelings of nostalgia and empathy. Each drabble brings out an interesting facet of the human predicament, sometimes ending with a twist, which is bound to leave the reader bemused. The drabbles by three authors have been presented as a potpourri for the reader to derive maximum reading pleasure from. Each drabble is signed off by the initials of the three authors, namely: BS, RR and IR respectively.

This collection has surprised us with the variations in the content and style of writing that have emerged from each of the three generations.

For the grandfather, who is now over ninety and has spent decades in the corporate world, the drabbles are mostly anecdotes from his workplace and relate interactions with colleagues and friends, tinged with humour.

The mother's canvas is largely created by observing and understanding her surroundings, people and their idiosyncrasies. One can see sensitivity and positivity in most of her drabbles. The stories play in the mind's eye as one reads them. Not only do they move the reader, but they also linger in our memory.

The daughter has been writing since the age of seven. Her first story (in its edited form) has been included in this book. Now, at the age of fifteen, during this difficult time of the pandemic, she has taken up the 'lockdown challenge' and has honed her skills in drabble writing. Besides, of course, conveying something meaningful and interesting in just a 100 words, this has involved the craft of editing. Writing them has taught her to say more using fewer and fewer words—as Shakespeare has said in *Hamlet*, 'brevity is the soul of wit!' Her drabbles are filled with imagination and are fictional.

These generational differences are thus quite evident in the manner in which we have selected our themes. Any person who loves reading will find our compilation interesting. We have kept our writing simple so as to reach out to a larger audience. We believe that it will particularly be a good way to encourage children to develop the habit of reading. We see many parents frustrated by the behaviour of their teenagers, hooked to computers or electronic games. However, when they try to suggest that their children pick up a book, they do not succeed. Books are usually lengthy and test the patience of a child. As this is a collection of 100-word stories, each story can be read in less than a minute and will be a perfect manner through which to bring children closer to books.

Other readers, such as those from older generations, will find the easy-reading drabbles a big relief.

We feel, that by getting the basic plot right, relaying it in a reader-friendly vocabulary and strictly maintaining the precision of 100 words has brought out the creative best in us as authors.

Happy reading!

1

Chee Chee

This event belongs to the period before the Chinese Revolution. The Chinese were westernizing, and the West, at best, was patronizing.

Dr Soong, Kuomintang's foreign minister, was seated beside an English grandee at an official dinner in London. Mylord didn't know that he spoke English. There was no conversation.

After soup, the Englishman, to be polite, turned to the yellow-man. 'Likee soupee?' Dr Soong smiled and nodded.

During the after-dinner speeches, Dr Soong was requested to speak. He delivered, much to his neighbour's discomfort, an excellent speech in flawless English.

As he sat down, he turned to Mylord, 'Likee Speechee?'

BS

2

～～～～～～～～～～～～～

The Rainbow Girl

'*A* for apple, B for ball...'

Bhagya repeats rhythmically. Her eyes brighten as I conduct the Rorschach Inkblot Test. The black ink card elicits the response: 'it is a rainbow, but the colours have faded!'

As the bell rings, she rushes out of school to join her friends. Raising the inflatable Minions up towards the clouds, she pauses by every waiting vehicle on the busy intersection. Winding up for the day, she looks up at the sky and sees an actual rainbow. Jumping with glee, she reaches her home, a shelter for street children, hoping tomorrow will be another day.

RR

3

~~~~~~

The Modern Mummy

The year was 1974. In the oppressive heat of Mexico City, a team of archaeologists were hard at work. The Great Pyramid was going to be dug up.

The coffin of the Pharaoh, enclosed, amidst walls full of hieroglyphics—it was a marvellous sight!

It was time to open the ancient coffin. The perfectly preserved mummy was adorned with sparkling amulets and jewels. But that was not what caught their attention. Tucked safely under the corpse was what appeared to be a mobile phone. 1973 had marked the invention of this gadget, 1974 was to mark its travel through time!

IR
~~~~~~

4

Longing

$\mathcal{A}$ long queue for water to be filled, a bickering in front of the common toilet, the women chopping vegetables—this very scene greeted me as I stepped into the premises.

Shantabai, an inmate of the home, moved closer to me and whispered, 'No one remembers... today is my birthday.' I embraced her and she clasped my hands tightly. Her wrinkled face and eyes full of longing seemed to be searching for someone... Almost reading my mind, she remarked, 'I am not waiting for my son's call. This is my home now.' Tears rolling down her cheeks, she hugged me.

RR

5

The Racy Drive

The holidays were growing dull and boring. I was driving nonchalantly. Suddenly, I caught a glimpse of her on the other side of the road. My heart started to pound as I moved towards her.

I had first been introduced to her in Boston; our hosts had shared amazing stories about her. True enough, she was different... something sweet and tart. In different hues, she looked so very inviting. It was love at first sight. Well, the memories of our first date were still vivid in my mind.

And here we were, face to face–my frozen yoghurt and I!

RR

6

Terra Incognita

Friday, 13th March, 2015. I was travelling to Alaska on the largest passenger plane ever known. With a weight of 240 tonnes, it zoomed loudly. The flight was to take an entire day. Most challenging of all was that I was travelling alone.

Everything was smooth, when suddenly, extreme turbulence hit us. The pilot had lost control. We were given parachutes for an emergency landing. I was petrified. I tried to remember an old joyride–in a hot air balloon. I landed on alien territory. I found myself surrounded by innumerable Lilliputians. It was the land of Lilliput! I fainted.

IR

7

Call of the Wild

*W*ith bated breath, Naivasha waited quietly, watching the migration of wildebeests through the ravines of Masai Mara. Millions of these animals crossing the Grumeti; a fascinating sight she had never before seen. A thump and a loud thud... many crossed over, escaping the eye of the wicked and cunning crocodile. But wait... what was that? The river turned blood red. A calf! Caught by the crocodile while the mother wildebeest watched in distress across the river. Naivasha heard the voice of God. Lo and behold! She jumped into the river, only to be united with the voice she had heard.

RR

How the Birds Got Their Colours

A snake went for a stroll in the forests of east Africa. Meandering deeper and deeper, he saw strange and colourful things.

'What are these?' he asked a mole.

'Flowers,' came the reply.

'How beautiful!' said the snake, and gobbled them all up.

'Why did you devour all the flowers?' complained the colourless birds.

'Because they looked nice.'

'But the forest no longer looks as nice!'

The snake considered for a moment and then shed its skin, unveiling different shades. Each bird took a colour; some preferred to remain black.

'Was this how the birds got their colours?' I wondered.

IR

Note: Written at the age of seven. I was studying in Cambridge, Massachusetts and was inspired by Rudyard Kipling's 'Just So Stories'.

~~~~~~~~~~~~~~~~~~~~~~~~~~~~~~

The Cheerleaders

*U*pon being asked what keeps me going as a cricketer, I invariably would answer: 'The fans.'

But now, with the pandemic, the stands were unusually devoid of the cheering crowd. 'So what if there are no "fans", we'll put air-conditioners in the stands,' my coach had joked.

Demotivated, I began practice. Unable to hit even a single shot, I was planning to retire for the day, when suddenly, I heard that familiar chorus. 'Sachin! Sachin!' It was music to my ears. Was I imagining things? Looking around the deserted stadium, I saw my team chanting my name, urging me on!

IR
~~~~~~~~~~~~~~~~~~~~~~~~~~~~~~

10

What Hurts Most

My friend, Malathi, a management consultant in her thirties was returning from Mussoorie with two male colleagues, after conducting a training programme. They were waylaid by laathi-bearing hoodlums. ' *Nikalo kya hai tumhare paas* .' Wallets were quietly handed over; rings, bangles and watches were snatched.

Malathi sat through the ordeal, nervous and apprehensive. Until one rogue came round to her side of the car and whispered, 'Don't worry, maataji. We only want money.'

Certainly, they were unscathed; the car was allowed to leave unhurt.

Malathi was livid, recounting the trauma to me. 'I can't imagine that oldie could call me *maataji!*'

BS

Note: '*Nikalo kya... paas*' or hand over everything you have; 'Maataji' or mother

Photo: Ruchi Ranjan

Eccentric Enigma

The hundred-year-old observatory could not withstand the test of time. Long ago, it used to have several irons in the fire. Now, the dilapidated building and a broken wooden staircase stood creaking; a testimony to the sheer neglect.

One morning, while walking through the campus, I found the usually deserted site brimming with activity. The watchman appeared frightened. He had seen a white, shrouded figure with frizzy hair walking up the steps of the observatory. The watchman became the butt of many jokes. But the lone cycle and the frizzy-haired wig, hidden away in the adjacent bushes, remained a mystery...

RR

12

The Birthday Spa

She sparkled in the bright sun. Spotless slate-coloured saree, one hand in mid-air, she waved to her admirers.

It was her special day, and she had bathed and scrubbed herself with the loofah. The long garland of fresh marigold flowers only added to her unmistakable charisma. After all, special days–birthdays–come only once in a year.

Standing tall, bidding au revoir to the sheen, waiting till next year for the special spa treatment, stood the imposing statue of the country's late prime minister. Until then, her crown would remain a free domain for pigeon poop and heaps of dust!

RR

13

Best Friend No More

The long wait was finally over. In five minutes, the clock would strike twelve, ushering in a year of new hopes, dreams and promises. The party was in full swing; the loud boisterous music enlivening the crowd. Looking across the bright dance floor, I glimpsed a very familiar face. She appeared to be my best friend from middle school. All agog, I ran and threw my arms around her, pulling her into a huge hug. I was flabbergasted when I was pushed towards a corner by my *best friend*. We stared at each other in disbelief. She was someone else!

IR

14

Ecstasy

The warmth of hot coffee and the smell of rain; Nia was in paradise. Wrapped up in a blanket, with her favourite book and dog curled up beside her, Nia was savouring the sugar cookies her mother had baked. Through the door, she could hear her father lightly strumming his guitar and humming a Beatles song. The sound of her mother's laughter mingled with the soft tones of the guitar, echoing through the house. This was one of those days when Nia was at her happiest, completely blissful, like a small child with not a single care in the world.

IR

15

Hide and Seek

Under the bed, below the table, behind the door; my entire family was playing hide and seek.

Social distancing and lockdown had limited our movement. He had to be somewhere! It was difficult to search for one located in a duplex. He refused to respond to our naïve calls. His silence complicated the operation.

Tempers ran high. Without him, work from home was impossible. And, during COVID-19, everything had to be done virtually... classes to webinars. Exhausted, I went to make a Pumpkin Spice Latte and reached for a cup and saucer. There lay silently... the hidden one... my smartphone!

RR

16

Metamorphosis

*S*hweta had moved to Cambridge, Massachusetts, with her seven-year-old daughter, Keya. It was a completely new environment! Keya would travel alone by the school bus. These were some of her motherly apprehensions.

Reaching the bus stop to pick up Keya, she was aghast to find it deserted. The bus had left without dropping her off. Trepidation writ large on her face, she took a cab to the last drop point. Tears rolling down her cheeks, fearing the worst, Shweta found her baby playing with the goofy caretaker. The caterpillar had morphed into a butterfly. Shweta wiped her tears and smiled.

RR

Photo: Ruchi Ranjan

Custodian of the Forest

'Hey! You... creatures...'

We looked down...

'Creatures! Who? We?'

'Yes, you... what brings you to this forest? I haven't seen anyone with books on this terrain.'

The members of a book lovers club were accosted by a strange sight. They had gotten together for an environment-related discussion. Suddenly, inching a little closer, it sniffed—like a dog. Finally convinced, it gave way and perched atop a nearby hillock, ready to be part of their group discussion. Bright orange, with a long black tail, this peninsular rock agama seemed to be the master and custodian of the undulating rocky forest cover.

RR

18

Flash of Lightning

There was a horse named Lightning. Its owner was a ruthless businessman, Jake. His servant, Ross, was a kind-hearted man, empathetic towards Lightning. Often, Lightning would refuse to run and as a punishment, Jake would starve it and lock it up for weeks altogether. Ross would secretly sneak in some food for Lightning. Many times, it tried to escape… but always in vain.

Once, when Jake was beating Lightning, Ross recorded the horrific act and replayed it for the cops. Jake was immediately arrested for animal cruelty.

Lightning now belonged to Ross, and true to its name, ran like lightning.

IR

Note: Written in the year 2014, when I was 10 years old.

The Musical Family

'It is dinner time!' she called out. A burly man, a tall girl and a stout boy entered. This was her family. 'Ooh! Wow! Butter chicken,' the son exclaimed. 'Let's dig in.' Grrr! The father reminded the family to say grace. Clink! A spoon fell. The daughter bent to retrieve it. Thud! She hit her head on the table. 'Ouch!' she loudly cried out as her brother laughed. Ding! It was the doorbell. Both siblings ran to answer it while the parents hoped that they would return after dinnertime.

This was the usual scenario at their bustling residence. Bon appétit!

IR

20

Prudence Jayate

The chairman of our Ceylonese subsidiary, Sir Cyril de Zoysa, was dreaded by his colleagues.

One morning, I found a clutch of directors from his companies in a fit of giggles. It so happened that Sir Cyril had barged out of the bungalow shouting, 'Why won't people leave my things alone? Now, where were my spectacles?'

Everyone was busy looking for the 'apparatus', but it was not to be found. Until they slipped to the nose from his knightly brow!

Certainly, everyone had seen the spectacles sitting there. But Sir had said they were missing, and none dared contradict him.

BS

21

Eggcelent

*I*t was larger than any other egg he had seen. This enormous egg at his father's coop did not seem ordinary. Whose could it be? James had to wait and watch.

This was almost a year ago. The egg had still not hatched. Suddenly, one bright morning, the egg cracked open. With an olive-green body, a single large eye and two antennae, this creature was the size and shape of a rather short human!

'Bazinga!' it exclaimed.

Screaming, James ran for his life. The strange creature followed. Cornering James, it held out an arm, extending an extraordinary hand of friendship!

IR

Google

Baithak of the Mynas

The mynas called for an emergency meeting in the Delhi University campus.

Muthu was in tears. 'I am ugly. Whenever college girls see me alone, they shoo me away... but are elated when Diku and I are together.'

Puzzled, the sarpanch of the myna clan ordered an enquiry and a reward for the one who could crack this mystery. Chunni, the youngest myna was tech-savvy. Surreptitiously, she pecked and opened the laptop of a student and hit search. A nursery rhyme dedicated to their clan—'one for sorrow, two for joy'—had been taken too seriously...

The reward was hers!

RR

Note: This story is based on an old superstition, according to which the number of mynas you see portends whether you will have good or bad luck. 'One for sorrow, two for joy,' is a traditional children's nursery rhyme about magpies (otherwise called mynas); 'Baithak' or a meeting.

23

Dare to be Different

$\mathcal{P}$ia felt unhappy that her name started with a 'P'. One more day, trudging after a sleepless night, tension looming before her viva-voce examination! The fifty students were divided into two groups, alphabetically. Names with A–O had been called on the first day.

All the students were flaunting their practical files—beautifully decorated chart paper covers—with the aim of impressing the external examiner.

Pia's turn. She answered the questions correctly. But why had she put a newspaper cover on her file, was the examiner's last question. Pat came the confident girl's reply, 'I want to be different, Sir.'

RR

24

The Battlefield

*I*t was a mass shoot-out. The enemy had been charging for a month and the agony continued. The attack grew more vigourous in the night. It appeared to be a battlefield, but a one-sided war. The enemy would come, see and conquer all. It had become a threat to their very existence, culminating in anxiety and sleeplessness.

The belief in Ahimsa had prevented me from using a single weapon against them. But now, no more. Their population was increasing and they were becoming a nuisance.

The kitchen table and drawers were crawling, full of them.

My battle-cry: 'Hail pest spray!'

RR

25

Dancing Queen

The sound of repairmen rendering final touches to her dilapidated tomb woke her from a deep slumber. Confronting them, she asked, 'What brings you here after so many years? Is Nizam Bahadur organising a mushaira and dance programme?'

'Yes...' the terrified workers could barely speak.

'Oh! It has been 186 years since I have put on my ghungroos,' she exclaimed, stroking her pet cheetah. The full moon lit her face. The night belonged to her, courtesan of the Deccan. Mah Laqa Bai Chanda stood elegantly as ever.

Before dawn, she disappeared as regally as she had arrived... in her palanquin.

RR

Note: Mah Laqa Bai Chanda was the first woman Urdu poet of the 18th century. She had participated in the three wars fought by the second Nizam of Hyderabad, dressed in male attire. Her tomb is located in Moula Ali, Hyderabad. *Mushaira* or a social gathering, often a contest of Urdu poetry; *ghungroos* or anklets.

26

A Whole New World

Our lives have been a lie! The experiments and satellite images were incorrect. Climate change had altered the face of the earth.

Going out of one's house is impossible. No, not because of the Coronavirus. This is something completely different. This is the end of everything we have ever known.

'Save yourself from a fall into oblivion by not stepping out. It's the end!' Live news flashed warnings.

After years and years of research, the Flat Earth Society finally rejoiced.

It had been proven that the earth is flat. It was time to see the world in a new shape.

IR

27

Good Vibes Only

The kaleidoscopic swirl of colours made her sit upright. The reflection of bright shades on the window mesmerised her. As the gale of wind rattled the glass, the windowpane danced to its tune.

The air was ripe with the fragrance of loamy earth and delicate blossoms. The pleasant, dewy petrichor smelt just heavenly.

Anika had been feeling low ever since she had been confined to bed. The accident had been unfortunate; a stroke of bad luck. It had restricted her mobility. Holding her crutches, she mustered the courage to stand and took a deep breath. Healing had only just begun.

RR

28

Real vs. Reel

Following the stream of black smoke, we departed from the road. Julia and I soon found ourselves surrounded by a dense forest. The cloud of impenetrable murky smoke led us to a decrepit house. The steady flame wasn't being tended to at all. Two burnt skeletal bodies lay outside. We had to act! Fast, frantically, we ran in search of aid. The sound of a running river guided us to a throng of people. How could they be so oblivious to the raging fire so near them? Angered, we confronted them. We were left red-faced. It was a movie shoot!

IR

The Wider Lens

Having failed his engineering exams, Suraj was shattered. Life had no meaning and he wanted it to end.

Deep in thought, he sat on the shore, gazing at the birds and the 'sun going down'.

Setting up his DSLR camera, he captured the image. The sight of a bird encapsulated in the 'ring of fire', appearing to break free, shook him completely. Like the bird, he imagined himself soaring–high above the sun. Gone were the days when he would sit alone and brooding.

Photography had always been his passion, and in an instant, he found new meaning to life.

RR

30

Wait for God

In the course of a naval exercise, the captain of a ship made a hash of the job, in fact denting a barge on the coast. This was a grave offence, deserving penalty, not to mention dirty looks from the crew of the dented barge.

Sweating and waiting for a severe reprimand, he was extremely relieved when a flash came from the command ship: Good.

Other ship officers were surprised but glad on their colleague's behalf. Champagne was being brought out and celebrations had begun. Until another flash struck: Apropos preceding message... after the word 'Good', add the word 'God'.

BS

The Whistle, A Boy

I began to retrace my steps to the car park. Early morning walks were very relaxing for me. This particular Saturday, the forest walking area appeared desolate. A cool wind blew and I enjoyed the breeze. Suddenly, I felt a shiver run down my spine. I didn't have the nerve to look back. Whistling sounds at regular intervals and I was all prepared to launch into a karate chop, lest things turned ugly. Nobody came closer. My speed had doubled by then. As I looked up in exasperation, perched atop a short tree, was the *whistling schoolboy*. I grinned sheepishly.

RR

Note: The Malabar whistling thrush is also known locally by the name of whistling schoolboy for the whistling calls that it makes. These calls have a very human quality.

32

Playing with Panthers

*T*he year was 1995. A villager entered the camp office of the Nandyal SDM, holding panther cubs. 'I found them deserted on the road, Sahib,' he announced. The SDM summoned the forest officials.

Meanwhile, milk from the feeding bottle and mutton pieces were offered to the cubs. No sooner had we bonded, that it was time to bid them adieu. The authorities ferried them to the zoo.

Six months later, we visited our babies. Smiling and waving, we stood in front of the cage. At their end, the big babies purred, as if to say, 'Thank you, we miss you!'

RR

Believe It or Not

Chaube ji's house in Mathura had become a cynosure of all eyes. People had gathered from everywhere to catch a glimpse. Whoever had heard by word of mouth was there in full attendance. They were standing there, wide-eyed, whispering and gasping in disbelief. 'Hmm... how is this even possible. No, it must be an imposter.' Sitting under the old Banyan tree, on a charpoy in a colourful dress, was a four-year-old girl, Shanti Devi.

Err... four-year-old or the illustrious wife?

Shanti Devi had come all the way from Delhi in search of her husband from her previous birth—Chaube ji!

RR

34

The Guest

Waking up in the morning to the sound–Kai Kai–I was amazed to see crows flying in the direction of the Neem tree in our backyard. Grandma's prophecy about crows cawing implied the arrival of guests. This proved true in a roundabout way. Perched on the tree was an owl that seemed to have lost its way. But for now, it was cornered.

Taking the saying '*athiti devo bhava*' literally, my family felt it was our bounden duty to protect it. Till dusk, we took turns to shoo the crows away. Later, the owl winked gracefully and flew away.

RR

Note: '*Kai Kai*' or the sound made by a crow; '*athiti devo bhava*' or the Guest is God.

35

Trapped

It was a dark, stormy night. The streets were flooded with rainwater. Not a single soul was in sight. Dhruv was standing at the foot of the hills, surrounded by a lush green forest. The ghastly shadows of the swaying trees were illuminated by the light of the moon. Standing in front of a deserted manor, Dhruv was cold and drenched. With no other choice, he entered the manor. The hair on the back of Dhruv's neck stood up. He felt as though there was someone else in there. Suddenly, he heard a loud bang...

BAM! The door locked shut.

IR

Pawsome

$\mathscr{D}$arjeeling calling! A beautiful valley surrounded by snow-capped peaks—the scene was breathtaking. The students were all set to trek through the Phalut.

Sounds of laughter mingled with the chirping of birds, crickets and grasshoppers, interrupting the peace and serenity of the eastern Himalayas. Upward and forward, it was a treacherous climb, but these students were not likely to give up. They made light of their situation by singing. Suddenly, they heard a soft bark. It was their school's pet, Laila. Turning back, they saw her nestling an injured owlet. Truly, a dog's love is the purest form of love.

IR

37

Midnight Rendezvous

It was way past midnight and the continuous buzz of the doorbell woke me from a deep slumber. Rubbing my eyes, I peeped out of the window to find that it was raining heavily.

Scared, I managed to ask loudly, 'Who is it?'

There was no answer. The ringing persisted. I opened the door very slowly, but found no one. Perplexed, I bolted the door and ran inside; white, as if I had seen a ghost.

Standing on a chair, my twelve-year-old daughter, Keya, was efficiently removing the battery from the 'conky' doorbell. There was pin-drop silence. Finally, peace prevailed!

RR

Photo: Debabrata Biswas

38

Snakes and Ladders

The mantra for success had been ingrained in him since childhood. He had been taught to be ahead of all others in a competitive world. Be it drama, sports, music or academics, Rohit was always numero uno. The word 'failure' had no place in his dictionary.

Rohit grew up to be a successful businessman. He had the Midas touch and the business flourished. But one day, the unimaginable happened. The stock market crashed and Rohit lost everything. He was shattered. Not used to failure, he had taken a steep fall from the ladders of success. The snakes were looming large!

RR

~~~~~~

Adventures for the Young

*S*creams and shouts greeted Keya at Hyderabad's adventure park. The eleven-year-old felt a rush of adrenaline.

As she got onto the Spin Ride, a voice from behind her exclaimed, 'Yay! Woohoo! Let us all go–' but it was cut short.

The seats filled up. Keya was thrilled. She moved on to the next ride. Again, there was a voice from behind; this time a complaint, a childlike burst, cribbing, 'I also want to. Nothing will happen.'

I turned back to see childhood revisiting Keya's aged grandma. The stick and the wheelchair were pushed to a corner by the beaming granny!

RR
~~~~~~

40

Meri Ganga Maili

$\mathcal{I}$t is not only now that the Ganga is maili. The story travels long back.

Mark Twain was shown round the holy town of Varanasi (the then Banaras). He was much impressed by the splendour of the ghats and the devotion of the bathers. But he remained unimpressed by the river.

'Rather dirty, the river, isn't it?'

'Oh, Sir, this is the holy Ganga, worshipped by many.'

'Filthy all the same.'

'Sir, people from far away come here for the holy water. It keeps for ages. No bacteria live in it.'

'Indeed. No self-respecting bacteria will ever live in it.'

BS

Note: '*Meri Ganga Maili*' or my Ganga, the river, is dirty.

41

Role Reversal

'Where is my pencil...'

'I too can't find my water bottle...'

Someone in the class had been stealing things. The teacher knew who it was. But, scolding him would have been futile.

The school's annual day preparations were on. The teacher had planned a small skit for her class. That day, all the children, including Chandu, were very excited because roles were being assigned. The skit was about a thief and the police. Chandu was a bright boy and good at acting. The teacher gave him the role of a policeman.

Chandu was a changed boy from the next day!

RR

42

The Yeti

*S*tanding across the road at a safe distance of six feet away, Annie waved frantically to her long-lost friend. Her enthusiasm was not reciprocated. Feeling dejected, but still hopeful, she ran to cross the road. To her utter disbelief, she was pushed away with powerful sprays of disinfectant.

'Why such strange behaviour?' Annie was appalled.

Puzzled, her friend said, 'Who are you? I don't know you.'

Looking at her reflection in the salon window, Annie saw the Yeti staring back at her. Salons had not opened yet. Three months of quarantine had given her the appearance of this powerful legend!

IR

43

School Alone

I was late. But what was that? Was everyone else late too? The school was deserted. Like the blazing sun above, my panic reached its zenith. I scrambled up the stairs, looked into all classrooms, laboratories and was met with the same sight. Where was everybody?

In the lab, surrounded by skeletons and dead animals, I felt something move. Goosebumps rose on my skin. Finally, mustering the courage to turn around, I heard a bark. Our school's pet seemed like an angel sent from heaven for me.

The calendar behind me depicted the date in red ink. Solved the mystery!

IR

Photo: Ruchi Ranjan

44

Standing Firm

*H*anging precariously in the air was the petiole of the Traveller's Palm tree. Ruby had been watching it every day, waiting for it to snap off. Surviving rough weather—heavy rainfall and strong winds, the sturdy petiole stood intact, all but a tiny crack.

One quiet morning after the storm had passed, Ruby found it lying on the ground. She looked at it closely. It appeared like birds soaring high. She picked it up, admired its courage and resilience. Fighting till the very end! Twenty-five years thence, it still adorns the walls of her living room—implanting hope and positivity.

RR

45

Mister Sinister

*J*ust as I settled into the backseat with my baggage, the driver's face flashed in the rear view mirror. The face looked just like one I had noticed on the news for the past few days. Fidgeting with my phone, I tried to dial the emergency number. Screech went the breaks! The phone flew out of my hands, under the front seat. Panicking, I reached for the door, then the windows... but they wouldn't budge. My 'driver' flashed a sinister smile and exited the freeway.

'Dead body found in an abandoned car. Culprit is on the loose,' the day's news read.

IR

The Early Riser

$\mathcal{J}$ust as he aimed to retrieve their watches from his sister, she teased, 'Go, buy new ones.'

Phew! There was little Gopi and Nimmo could do. They had to rush to the airport.

Landing at Cairo, they headed to their friend's house. Rise and shine—the glare of the scintillating sun woke them early the next morning. Curious about the time, they sneaked around the quiet 'clockless' house.

Two hours of uncertainty finally ended. The doorbell rang. Yawning away, their hostess appeared. 'What is the time?' Gopi jumped to enquire.

'The sun wakes early in Cairo,' she muttered, still sleepy.

RR

47

Life Can Never be the Same Again

'Chana jor garam, babu, mai laaya mazedaar...' sang the hawker on his spree.

Gone were the days when Vikram would smell the paper cone brimming with chana. He was now a public figure, followed continuously by gunmen for his security.

One night, Vikram, in guise of a commoner, sneaked out to enjoy street food. The simple pleasures of life, away from his retinue, were sheer bliss. Popping masala chana, Vikram smelt the paper cone, nostalgic about his carefree days. The oil-soaked newspaper cone was a spoilsport... carrying his photograph, suited and booted. All he could manage was a wry smile.

RR

Note: 'Chana jor garam, babu, mai laaya mazedaar...' or Sir! I have brought tasty and hot black gram. Masala chana or spicy black gram.

48

Animal Empire Strikes Back

The park was the city's breather. Full of trees, it was a paradise on earth. The youth jogged, children played and the elderly leisurely strolled. What more? The peacocks, squirrels, birds, mongoose, porcupines and the trees lived in harmony.

Last Sunday, visitors to the national park were in for a shock. The main gate was locked. All the animals and birds had formed a barricade, an 'animal chain', protesting against the upcoming debacle at the park. The 'giving trees' were to be axed. It was time the animals took stock of the situation, demanded they be heard and taken seriously!

RR

49

Against All Odds

$\mathcal{K}$arishma was a child prodigy, a gift from God. She was able to speak four languages fluently by the age of three. But, Karishma's life was not a bed of roses.

It was her sixth birthday and her family was headed to the Natural History Museum. A severe blizzard struck. Two significant lives were lost; Karishma was orphaned. The 1993 'Storm of the Century' had 208 fatalities. For Karishma, it turned her life upside down.

Fighting against all odds in the orphanage, Karishma strived as hard as ever.

Today, the founder of the fastest-growing multinational, Karishma never fails to inspire.

IR

50

Deep Sea Terror

It was a cold morning. Vacationing in Mauritius, I had planned to go scuba-diving. Decked up in a diving suit, flippers and carrying an oxygen tank, I was ready for an adventure.

Splash! I jumped in. Exploring the habitat of sea creatures, I suddenly saw an unidentifiable creature heading my way. Petrified, I began swimming at full-speed towards the boat.

The strange fish was already there before me! Instinctively, I screamed for help. The guide who had come to my rescue, burst out laughing. 'It's our local dolphin,' he said, bemused. Chuckling, we all swam elegantly with the intelligent creature.

IR

51

Detox

$\mathcal{A}$ tough nut, they say, is hard to crack. It was growing difficult to understand or deal with him. From yellow to black, his character was becoming tarnished.

My orthopaedic friend advised: he needed to be uprooted from the bed due to his irregular growth and behaviour.

Brooding, I cast a forlorn figure standing outside the doctor's door. One glance at my pedicured feet and I could see the paint camouflaging the blackness of the toe nail. But, this was transient.

It was time to detox. I twisted open the nail paint remover bottle. At last, he could breathe easy!

RR

52

Forever Young

The face in the mirror was not his. It was more handsome, more vibrant, glowing and young as ever. He frowned dubiously, but his reflection smiled.

Soon he would be under the needle. Uncertainty consumed him. There was not much time left to back out. How could he do this to himself? His reflection smiled at him approvingly, but the shoulder-perching angel said otherwise. He stared blankly at the mirror. SMASH! The glass broke into thousands of pieces. Ignoring the excruciating pain coursing through his right hand, he strode out of the clinic. Age reduction surgery was not for him.

IR

As Bright as the Fireflies

Flowering cherry trees, a lush green meadow, a hilly countryside–the view was breathtaking. But where were the country's children? Fourteen long hours at school, Sanghi's life was tough. There was neither time to play nor bound through the open fields.

Growing up in a poor family, where her parents could not even afford the oil-based petromax lantern, she remained undeterred.

During power-cuts, the family would catch many fireflies and put them into a glass jar. Sanghi would study under that light, come what may. The adage 'where there is a will, there is a way' was her life's motto.

RR

Much Ado About Nothing

The mercury rose to 103 degrees Fahrenheit. No, this wasn't the afternoon temperature of Hyderabad, but Keya's body temperature.

Tests indicated that she had dengue, the bone-breaking fever. The paediatrician assured that it was self-limiting. Only, her platelet count required continuous monitoring. The advice of well-wishers to consume papaya leaf juice—a quick remedy—convinced me to try it. The whole exercise, from plucking the leaf to grinding it, was very exciting for Keya. But all efforts to cajole her into taking a teaspoonful proved futile. She ran like the wind.

And the next morning, the platelet count shot up!

RR

55

The Precious Pearl

Her cheeks were wet. She gazed upwards. It was raining heavily but she had an umbrella for protection. Nothing had fallen into her eyes either. She brought her little finger to the cheek to see what it was. Very gently, she raised it. It was a translucent globule—a valuable pearl, too precious to be wasted like that. Wondering how it had leaked out of her box of treasures, she pulled herself upright. She could feel the presence of an invisible force embracing her, lending a strong shoulder. Life is too short for sadness; life is too short for tears!

RR

Challenged by Covid

Dressed in my protective COVID gear—gloves and a mask—I headed to work. Today's meeting was very important. With the presentation slides secure in my iPhone, I was feeling quite confident.

Maybe, I would finally land that promotion. But fortune revealed other plans.

I looked at my phone, waited for the Face Recognition to work, but alack! I decided to try the Touch Identification instead, but in vain. I frantically tried to guess my passcode...

'My birthday? My dog's birthday? 1234?'

Taking on the impromptu challenge, I began my speech, extempore. Applause filled the air. The promotion was mine!

IR

Photo: Rahamtul Haq

Daughters as Daughters

*U*ndaunted, she drove all the way to the Godavari river bath. In their patriarchal set-up, which predominantly eulogized on the birth of a son, here was a daughter taking charge.

Transcending the taboos imposed by society, she carried the earthen pot of her father's ashes for immersion. Keeping herself afloat on the wobbly coracle, she held on to the pot. The boat paused in the middle of the river. With a heavy heart, she let it go.

Life comes full circle. She moved ahead: a snail on the shore, back bearing a tough exterior. She was down but not out.

RR

58

Bruno's Day Out

It was a chilly day. Bruno was more restless than ever. 'Mummifying' the whole house with toilet paper, he was now plotting his next mischief. I decided to take Bruno to the park.

'Fetch!'

Bruno ran behind the ball. But he returned with a bone instead. The bone was etched with mysterious carvings. It was not a regular bone.

We walked towards the police station. The overcast sky predicted rain.

Suddenly, the bone began to glow. A burst of lightning struck. Astonished, I dropped it. More lightning flashed. In the blink of an eye, the bone had disappeared. I shuddered.

IR

59

Knock Knock

Enveloping the balcony of his house was the guava tree with its long branches. Amidst the cacophony of life, Yuvi had little time to stand and appreciate the invigorating calls of birds on the tree.

But he would often sneak a look at the sparrows building a nest in his balcony. Food was always kept aside for them before he left for school. One day, he forgot.

The silence of the house upon his return was broken by a couple of knocks. The glass door overlooking the balcony reflected the sparrows, pecking and scolding him. 'Where's our food?' they cried.

RR

60

Machines May Lie

$\mathcal{K}$ishan, my classmate, nurtured his self-image as a ladies' man. More so with the 'luck' on the card from the stand-up weighing machine, proclaiming: 'You pose extraordinary attraction for the opposite sex.'

This was, of course, immediately announced on public domains. But Kishan's sights were actually on the girls in the class. Specially Surjeet.

Catching up to her, ostensibly for lecture notes, their conversation turned to the importance of Body Mass Index, leading up to the precious card, handed over, 'inadvertently', the wrong side up. Surjeet, bemused, looked at both sides, observing: '*Iss me tumhara wazan bhi galat lagta hai.*'

BS

Note: '*Iss me... lagta hai*' or your weight, too, seems to be wrong here.

61

Short-Cut

Clad in her glittering saree with the golden danglers, she waited at the station with her better half. The metro arrived.

Her hair fluttered as she sat in the autorickshaw hired at the last station. Good Lord! Stuck in a heavy traffic jam! She saw herself following her husband on foot—in her Prada heels. Phew!

Reaching the wedding, they heard stories from the other guests about being caught in traffic snarls for over two hours.

With a look of contentment on his face, the hubby chuckled, 'It took us just half the time!'

The 'celebrity couple' left everyone wonderstruck.

RR

Photo: Ruchi Ranjan

The Director's Cut

'Lights, Camera, Action–'

'–Cut' yelled the movie director. Curious morning walkers had paused to watch a movie being filmed. The location was a school, housed in a heritage building. In one section, classes were in progress. The director's command to stop came as a surprise to the crew. There was pin-drop silence. Reverberating across the air, rang out a melodious voice.

'*Aye malik tere bande hum*,' the voice rose from one of the empty classrooms. The singer was a mentally-challenged girl. It was a school for the specially-abled. Clapping, the crew entered the class. The girl was overjoyed.

Note: '*Aye malik tere bande hum*' or Oh lord, we are your servant

RR

63

Dead Man Alive

'He's been dead for ten years,' the old lady remarked, looking at me with grave concern.

Mrs Osborne, a sweet lady in her seventies, had come to invite to her house-warming ceremony. When she laid eyes on me, she gasped loudly, clutching her heart as though she had seen a ghost.

Mrs Osborne had been my neighbour for only a few months. It turned out that I bear a striking resemblance to her late son. Well, now she has found her son! As they say, there are at least seven people in this world who may well be your doppelgangers.

IR

64

Whose Script Is It?

*H*unched over my manuscript, I tried to make sense of my previous chapters. These were not my words—I had written something completely different. But how could this have happened? The manuscript hadn't left my sight since I had begun.

'Danger, danger everywhere,' the words read. Were the words conveying a message? I must read between the lines. Was this a warning? Lost in thought, I gazed out of the window, when suddenly, more words started to appear on the script.

'Ghost-writing in its purest form,' it scrawled.

Black Magic and the Paranormal was the new title of my novel.

IR

Photo: Ruchi Ranjan

The Solitary Window

The solitary window stood, a silent spectator. The only thing that had changed during the last fifty years was the paint... from bright green to dull grey.

'*Malai, Aam, Pista ki kulfi le lo...*' The heavy, husky lure of the kulfiwala made me stretch my arm to unlatch the creaking window.

The image hadn't faded—the vendor, a matka on his head, walking through this gully of old Delhi, the abode of my grandparents many years ago. And standing amidst the ruins was this window, which had withstood the test of time, many stories nesting in its rusty hinges.

RR

Note: '*Malai, Aam... le lo*' or buy cream, mango, pistachio ice-cream; 'matka' or an earthen pot

66

Masked

When Tia and Ben met and courted, they thought they were made for each other. Soon they were married. Tia's idyllic world turned upside down when she discovered that he resembled Stevenson's Dr Jekyll, turning into Mr Hyde. There were two sides to Ben's personality... behind the respectable facade lurked dark secrets. Ben was nasty to Tia. He would rationalise his behaviour, which only served to disguise the real reasons for such conduct.

Lying down on the Freudian couch in the therapist's clinic, repressed childhood experiences were brought to the surface and resolved.

Ben and Tia lived happily ever after.

RR

~~~~~~~~~~~~~~~~~~~~~~~~~~

Trick or Treat

*M*y head was throbbing. My vision blurred. Where was I?

'HELP!' I screamed.

It seemed like I was inside a crate with no way out. I could hear the sound of wheels rolling underneath. Where was I being taken to—under captivity? Who was my abductor? Giving up all hope, I closed my eyes, waiting for death to greet me. Suddenly the lid of the crate opened. Familiar faces, amidst them a furry one, looked down at me, filling me with comfort.

'Birthday escapade!' they shouted out. Good things demand patience... and kidnapping! The adorable puppy was the best gift.

IR
~~~~~~~~~~~~~~~~~~~~~~~~~~

68

The Walls of Silence

Breaking the walls of silence, they rushed into the park, full of morning walkers. They ran, jogged and laughed. Inhaling the fresh air, they gazed around, experiencing nature's bounty. Sunday mornings were keenly awaited by these children. Indulging in playful banter, each tried to run faster than the other.

Suddenly, one of the boys stopped mid-gait. He had collided into a headphone-clad walker, scrolling through his phone. Engrossed in sound, he was oblivious of his surroundings. The observant boy apologised in sign language. The walker became speechless and gestured at the boy. The interplay of 'talking hands' looked so ironic!

RR

69

Enhancing the Taste

My friend and his cousin, Brij and Rajbans, were posted in Mathura, sharing Brij's bungalow with the family retainer, Chandan, as house-help. Chandan was a good housekeeper and cook. Except that the whisky in their bottles diminished faster than they imbibed it.

To teach Chandan a lesson, they bought a bottle of Ballantine. They emptied it, pissed in it and put it back. The level reduced although they were, sensibly, consuming none of it. Time to accost Chandan!

Chandan was unfazed: '*Sahib, mai toh peeta nahi. Bas do chimche aapke soup me roz daal deta hoon. Swad ke liye.*'

BS

Note: '*Sahib, mai... ke liye* ' or Sir, I don't drink. I only put a spoonful or two into your soup to enhance the taste.

Finding the Warrior Within

Despite studying engineering from a prestigious college, Arjun was unhappy. He was caught in a dilemma. The rift between his parents' expectations and his own aspirations was ever widening. Afraid of going against their wishes and the consequent conflict, he had joined the college.

While Arjun managed to clear his exams, towards the last semester his tolerance had reached a final threshold. All these years, music had been his only solace. He was now determined to follow his passion.

'Dad, I am going to be a musician,' he said with conviction. Arjun was beginning to do justice to his name!

RR

The Byte

*E*ureka! After two years of painstaking effort, we had finally achieved the impossible. Teleportation would soon be the new normal. But there was a 'bite-sized' problem...

Our team had been successful in teleporting an apple into the orbit—a major feat indeed—but the apple had reappeared with a strange and rather large bite mark!

'Aliens!' was the first thought that came to my mind. Looking up at the clear glass dome, I saw a strange figure shadowed. Being a physicist, I didn't believe in the E.T. or the paranormal. But this was unbelievable! Were they coming to get us?

IR

The Mesh of Strings

Strewn everywhere, littering the streets, lay the tattered kites. Just a day before, it was a different scene altogether. The sky was dotted with colours, and everyone was engaged in a kite flying frenzy.

The abrasive manja used to fly kites had been claiming the lives of many helpless birds every year. And this year was no exception.

Two good Samaritans had climbed atop a tree to save a pigeon tangled in the deadly manja. Though they were able to save it, the helpless bird was forced to remain caged. It had clipped wings for the rest of its life.

RR

Note: Manja or the glass powder coated kite flying and fighting string.

73

Dark

The whole world turned black. Was I unconscious? Or was this a dream? Slowly, I raised my arm, then attempted to pinch myself. Ouch! My mind was foggy. Trudging ahead through the dark maze, I crashed into several obstacles. Stumbling, I reached 'heaven'. My source of divine light lay in front of me. But what was this mysterious object radiating such bright light? The sun? No, it must be the moon.

As I reached the balcony, my mother flashed the torch at my face. There was a power-cut! The past week's sleepless nights had finally taken its toll on me.

IR

Dev and His Companion

She was his constant companion, loyal and dedicated to the core. In times of joy and sadness, she provided true and unconditional love, rarely seen even in human beings. The four-legged Julie and the two-legged Dev were inseparable. With very few friends of his own breed, my grandfather's house was the only abode they visited.

Life is full of twists and turns... Dev succumbed to a strange illness, leaving Julie all alone. Not sure if she understands what has happened, but her daily visits to my grandfather's house continue. She searches each and every room with a sad, vacant look.

RR

Building Blocks

Seemingly unmindful of the events happening around him, Nirav was immersed in building models with his set of Lego blocks. The day's news flashed on the television... twenty-two dead in the Manchester blast; child killed in shooting at elementary school...

The house was decked in New Year's festivity when Nirav's cousins arrived from India. Playing together, some started drawing and colouring on sheets; Nirav hurriedly wrote something.

It struck a chord in my heart when I saw what had been written: 'I want peace in the country when I become the President'. This is what the precocious four-year-old had scribbled.

RR

Never Give Up

$\mathcal{T}$he ball hit the table. Ron cheered loudly. Table tennis had always fascinated him. He was an ardent follower of the game, a walking-talking encyclopaedia regarding all the matches played nationally and internationally.

Neither rain nor storm could deter him from going to the table tennis academy each day after school. With a keen eye, he would observe the other players and follow every move of the ball.

After the 'regular players' finished, Ron stood up to play. There was only a single difference. He played the game holding the paddle in his mouth. He had lost both his hands.

RR

The Ritual

There was laughter and chatter all around. Suddenly, he took out a sharp instrument. Holding it to the throat, he was all set to start. Cries of panic echoed through the hall. No one came to the rescue. The silence of the spectators was most disturbing. Sweet nothings did not help either.

The torturous process finally ended. With tears in her own eyes, the relieved mother took the baby in her arms and hugged her. Turmeric was applied on the tonsured head.

The baby saw herself in the mirror and laughed loudly. 'Wow! Two-two babies' she seemed to be saying!

RR

<hr>

Holding On

$\mathcal{T}$he tap of the spoons on the katoris sounded like a Jaltarang. Ramu had only these vessels to play with. His father, a balloon seller, left home every evening to sell his wares. The colourful balloons brought a sparkle to Ramu's eyes. But he knew, each balloon sold meant food for the night.

Accompanying his father one evening, he watched the children in the park clamouring for balloons. 'I want blue... I want orange...' One by one, all the balloons except for one, were sold. Hands held tightly, they walked home. The sparkle in Ramu's eyes was bright as ever.

RR

Note: 'Katori' or a steel bowl; 'Jaltarang' or a melodic percussion instrument, originating from the Indian subcontinent

Shop Right

$\mathcal{S}$arah screamed, clinging to the steep mountain edge with all her might.

Her father had warned her, but she had paid no heed. After all, this was the 25th century. Anything and everything was possible today. She had heard about the mundane things her ancient ancestors had done. It had all sounded so boring.

With a lust for adventure, Sarah was what you would call a 'modern daredevil'.

But now, her death was imminent. There was no hope. If by any chance, she survived, she would have to admit that her dad was right. Never buy generic discounted anti-gravity boots.

IR

Necklace or Noose?

It was the most alluring heirloom. Intricate carvings of phrases from the Bible ornamented the pendant. Today, this precious antique was finally mine. Alone in the Herefordshire hills, I set out on my solitary hike. The necklace adorning my neck grew tighter with every breath. Soon it was choking me. Eerie sounds echoed through the hills. The cawing of ravens rang over my shrieks. No matter how hard I tried, it wouldn't come off. An enormous Banyan tree loomed in the distance. Hundreds of bodies hung from the branches of the tree—each dangling with a necklace similar to mine.

IR

The Silent Night

The grandfather clock struck... DONG! It was twelve. Midnight. I woke up to a sound... thap-thap. Somebody was trying to break open the door.

Terrified, I covered myself with the blanket. There was a pause. Then, it started again. I shuddered. In the quiet of the night, the sound was shrill and piercing.

I edged my way slowly in its direction and asked, 'Who is it?' There was no response. The sound grew louder and louder. I moved ahead and found myself standing in the bathroom. Wiping the beads of sweat off my forehead, I tightened the dripping water tap.

RR

#Instafamous

*O*ver two million Instagram likes, a thousand Facebook reactions and many appreciative comments on WhatsApp; the picture was worth a thousand words.

During the COVID-19 pandemic, with no other means of entertainment, the sight of this South Korean beauty lent a refreshing aura. Social media was going gaga, and she felt that she was the trendiest, the best company one could have during the quarantine. Her sweet, cool looks and she came with a swagger on top.

While the Corona curve was not flattening, her popularity curve kept rising.

Introducing the modern version of our '*desi phenti hui coffee*'... Dalgona!

RR

Note: '*desi phenti hui coffee*' or local whipped coffee.

<hr>

The Mysterious Mr Red

*H*e stood in a corner wearing a red dusty overcoat and a red beanie. Long forgotten, he had caught the attention of a few Gen-Z children playing around. They were amused. 'This black gaping mouth seems to have a secret passage. But it is locked. Let's drop a stone and hear it,' they whispered excitedly. It plopped inside making a hollow sound. Just then, a man in khaki appeared and started to open the lock. They peered in. 'Five letters in this big robust body!' they exclaimed in unison.

The instant click—Sent!—had replaced the 'plop' of posted letters.

RR

More Than a Home

*S*heltered within the seafront cafe, we watched the storm fade away. Raging with fury, it had hit this city of Tahiti like a rampant mob.

Watching tourists, vendors, families, pets—everyone run from the pier, I was filled with a sense of dread. There was chaos everywhere. I had experienced storms on the news and movies before, but witnessing such a calamity in real life made my head reel and stomach churn. Rather than retreating like any other tourist, I decided to help this city and its lovely people. An enigmatic city full of strangers somehow felt home to me.

IR

Paris Pre-empted

Ramesh, a young boy in his teens, was allowed a month's holiday in England by his affluent parents. Condition being: 'Stick to England; no travel to sin city, Paris.'

Paris, being taboo, naturally was predominant in Ramesh's plans.

Cleverly, he addressed three postcards to his mother, each dated at a week's interval. Aided by the Tourist Guide, they described his (imaginary) excursions in London and around.

These he handed over to the landlady, to post each, date-wise. And off to Paris.

But the puzzled landlady, seeing no point in delaying the job, put them all in the mailbox. ALL TOGETHER!

BS

86

Hope

Gazing out from the window, the sight of the sunset drew her into a pensive mood. Day 59 into the COVID lockdown—there was no hope.

Amidst the white clouds, she saw a grey monster, reminding her of the Coronavirus. 'Can't it be destroyed by the sun's intense heat?' she wondered. She had read that the virus perishes at high temperatures.

The red blooms brought a smile to her face. With a twinkle in her eye, the teenager strode towards the kitchen to try a new recipe from her menu of 'lockdown specials'... lockdown had given wings to her creativity!

RR